OMEGA FOR JEALOUS ALPHA

Wolf Shifter MPREG Fated Mates Romance

Michael Levi

ISBN: 9798421872368
Imprint: Independently published

1st edition

Cover design by: Michael Levi

CONTENTS

CHAPTER 1

Nefion

"Yeah, yeah. I'm going there in a bit," I said, looking away from my father. He was in the doorway, glaring at me. It was as though he was doing everything in his power not to kill me. I knew he was hiding something. That look in his eyes didn't fool me, after all.

I pulled up my backpack slightly, going to the bus stop. When I peeked over my shoulder, I couldn't see my father anymore. Thank goodness. Already 19 and I couldn't stop obsessing about this one thing – I needed to move out of my house and find my own place.

Perhaps an apartment in the middle of nowhere. Or in downtown, where I could hit all the gay bars and meet all kinds of different people. Make more friends. I had a lot of them now, but still, more wouldn't hurt.

I couldn't stop thinking of college. That Management degree was going to come in handy when I had it. For one, my uncle said he was going to hire me. My graduation gift and I couldn't wait until I had it. I'd be bossing everyone around, which was something that never happened in my college life.

Just because I was a little shorter than normal, people always assumed that I was supposed to be very submissive. Well, they didn't know anything about me.

I waved my hand over my head when I spotted some of my

friends at the bus stop. They were all giggling, chatting, and having a lot of fun. I couldn't wait until we were together and I was having fun with them, too.

The road by my side was packed with cars and motorcycles. I scrunched up my nose at the motorcycles, not liking them one bit. There was just something about bikes that was a turn-off. I smiled gently, thinking that my uncle would be flaying me alive right now if he knew that I thought that way about them.

He thought that everyone loved motorcycles, even though that couldn't be further from the truth. Most of the people that lived in the city thought that way about them, to be honest.

Urgh. I couldn't help but feel like punching them hard for thinking that way. Those motorcycles were polluting the streets, ruining everything, making a lot of noise, and generally making city life pretty unbearable. I just wanted them all gone. Was that something so hard to grasp?

I peeked behind my shoulder when I thought that a certain group of bikers was riding in this direction. Relieved that it wasn't them, I breathed out a sigh of relief. I was thinking that because of a certain rumor floating around. People at college were telling me that my parents were going to pair me with a biker, which couldn't be true.

Right behind the group of my friends at the bus stop was the guy I wanted. He was a couple of years older than I was and hot as balls. Just finding him with my eyes now, I couldn't stop thinking about him and it was pretty obvious that he thought the same way.

Not that I thought anything would ever happen. He hit on me sometimes, especially when we were partying or any time we had the opportunity to talk, but I didn't interact much with him. One of the reasons was that I was focusing on college right now and couldn't be distracted. I just didn't feel ready for a relationship. I didn't feel like having to give someone bucketloads of attention all the time, which was something that was a requirement for that.

I did feel a little bad that I couldn't tell my friends about my first time, though. I thought that I'd eventually find a guy that I was comfortable with, but all the people I knew in college were either rough bros that would certainly hurt me a lot or were too flamboyant. They didn't know this, but I had something for caring, older men, and I couldn't find that at the parties I went to.

I tried hooking up with my crush, but he said he wasn't interested. He said that he was looking for something more permanent, most likely already thinking about the person that he'd marry one day. The thought of getting married didn't cross my mind at all, and thus I couldn't help but feel that it was an alien concept to me. For the time being, anyway.

Although... Fuck. I couldn't stand even remembering that it was going to happen.

There was also the whole thing about fated mates that I couldn't wrap my head around. Who the hell was supposed to confirm that I was going to be someone's fated mate?

It didn't even make sense and, yet, the thing seemed to be trending right now. Apparently, that was happening because of a couple that found out they were always meant to be together and didn't know anything about it until it was too late. They were in an attack in a church somewhere in town.

Pushing that thought out of my mind, I couldn't help but feel that it was nothing more than an illusion. But it was a different kind of illusion, too. I didn't know this for sure, but I was thinking that I knew that couple. They were the ones in the mountain, weren't they?

I didn't know their full story – they kept it locked behind several doors – but they were Alpha and Omega, had a child, and I'd cared for it when I was a couple of years younger.

I couldn't help but hope that the same would happen to my life one day. I didn't think it ever would, though.

Seconds later, when I thought that I was going to be with my friends and maybe play around with my crush, I felt a strong hand pulling me back. I spun around, meeting the fervent eyes of someone I'd rather not see again.

He was glaring at me and I didn't like the look on his face. He always said that he'd rather see me alone than with someone else.

There was something about him that reeked. He was one of the 'Believers.' One of the people that thought that fated mates existed.

"What are you doing here, Palio?" I grumbled, folding my arms over my chest. As soon as everyone noticed that Palio was with us, they all went silent. I couldn't hear anything other than the cars and the motorcycles driving on the road.

I must've been so focused on spending quality time with my friends that I didn't even notice that he was coming in my direction. Taking a glance over his shoulder, I noticed his motorcycle parked by the sidewalk, the engine turned on. He thought that he wasn't going to have to spend a lot of time here.

"I thought I said I was going to take you to campus myself. I don't like it when you take the bus. It's not safe and you know that it's filled with sex offenders."

I took a look over my shoulder, realizing he was right about that, even if only in part. There were some shady people by the bus stop, but Palio didn't need to worry about them.

He was just being jealous. It wasn't the first time that this was happening. He thought that I was his fated mate and that, one day, we'd get married.

He was a biker. I couldn't help but take mental notes of the black inks on his skin. His tattoos. They defined his being, showed him the kind of person he was, and they made me wonder what his past was like.

He didn't have a lot of money, but he had influence in his motorcycle club. Palio was one of those guys. He felt that he didn't even need to wear a helmet, which was ridiculous and irked me.

I didn't like how he was still keeping me frozen in place with his hand. Not to mention that I could tell the bus was going to come soon and that I'd have to hop onto it. What was this guy thinking he was doing? Was he thinking he was going to throw me onto the seat of his bike and take me to college without my permission?

Things didn't work like that here... Or perhaps they did. I couldn't help but feel submissive in front of him, despite putting up a tough face and glaring back at him.

Palio was a head taller than me and a lot stronger. I didn't doubt that he could wipe the floor with me, though I was sure that was something that would never cross his mind. That he cared a lot about me was evident. I could see it in the way he looked at me, and I could tell that he wasn't going to budge about this, either.

I peeked over my shoulder, realizing that I wasn't going to be able to chat a little with Cynem. My crush was going to have to entertain himself with a girl that kept whoring herself for him, and I couldn't help but feel sorry.

I sighed and sat on Palio's bike. At least I was going to get to college earlier.

CHAPTER 2

Palio

The rumbling of the motorcycle's engine was like music to my ears. Happy that Nefion decided to come along, I twisted the handlebars of the motorcycle and rode off while everyone was staring at us.

They were asking themselves what was happening. If only they knew. I was with my fated mate and even though he always said he didn't want to have anything to do with me, I was pretty sure that his mind would eventually change about it.

He wasn't happy that he had to be hugging me from behind, his body pressed against mine. I was taking him to campus, where I would, unfortunately, have to part ways momentarily with him. I wanted to spend all the time I had with him, and my time was limited, just like everyone else's.

It was no secret that I wanted to spend as much time with him as possible.

I went through hell to find out that he was my fated mate and that we were supposed to marry. I couldn't wait until I was building a family with him, which was one of my dreams.

The wind was blowing against my face and I felt so free I didn't want to get off the bike.

Nefion put his head close to my ear before he said, "You do realize that the whole fated mates thing is ridiculous, right? It's not going to happen. You can't force me to marry you."

I turned my head to look at his eyes, loving how beautiful they were. They were looking right back. Nefion was anything but a coward, which was one of the attributes from him I most liked.

"You might think that way about it at the moment, but your mind will be changed soon. You can be sure of that."

He groaned, pulling his head back. "I'm only doing this because of my father. He has a very strong opinion about us getting married and… I don't want to disappoint him."

I could see where Nefion was coming from. His father was one of the most influential figures in his life and he was such a determined person that it even rubbed off on me. He was an example to be followed, I thought. One day, I was pretty sure that his stressful life would be no more and that he would open a very big smile at our wedding.

His son was mine and was also the most important person in the world for me, which was saying something. So many people marked my life and one day I would thank all of them.

I pulled over, Nefion getting off Destiny and pulling up his backpack. He was looking at me with curious eyes, making me wonder what was going on in his mind right now.

There was this pre-wedding party that we were going to. It was supposed to be a Valentine's Day party and I couldn't wait until I was going there with him. Nefion didn't like it, but I was pretty sure that his mind was going to change about it.

I didn't turn off the engine of the motorcycle. I wasn't coming back here to pick him up and take him home, even though that was something I'd like to do. His dad said that he was going to pick him up and I had to obey all of his wishes, that one included. After all, we were fated mates, but his father's wishes took precedence.

For now, anyway. I couldn't wait until we were living together and I didn't have to tell his parents about what we were doing.

Sniffing his scent, I couldn't help but feel the wolf side of me trying to come out. I wasn't going to let it do that, though. It was locked up inside of me, where it couldn't jump out and ruin my life. I like being a wolf shifter and I had some control over it, but I didn't like it when I wasn't my normal self anymore.

Nefion looked uncomfortable, shifting his weight. It didn't matter how he tried to hide it. The sexual tension between us was very strong and he couldn't conceal it. He couldn't even hide the feelings that he had for me. He knew that I was handsome, tall, and his type.

That was one of the many reasons why we were fated mates.

I approached him, halting when I was right in front of him. Putting my hand on his cheek, I brought his head up as we sealed our lips. We were kissing right in front of the college, where everyone was looking at us and giggling and making snarky comments.

I didn't pay much attention to them, focusing on this exquisite moment. His lips were just so sweet! I could see myself kissing Nefion for hours on end, if only that were possible. Nevertheless, I was very well aware that it wasn't and I was going to keep that in mind.

I didn't use my tongue, even though the kiss was a very passionate one. When I pulled my head back, I could see it in his eyes. He liked it. Nefion didn't want to admit it, but he liked the kiss and craved more.

He was even breathless, which was something that didn't happen often to someone that was on the track team. I took a step backward, still feeling his smell. His scent was something I would always remember. Everyone had a scent and it was always very characteristic and distinctive.

"You shouldn't have kissed me in front of everyone. That wasn't cool."

That was what he was saying, but I knew that it didn't mean anything. He liked it so much that he was just toying with me. Seeing that, I couldn't help but smile.

"It will never happen again. I promise," I affirmed, getting back on my bike and twisting the handlebars. The engine rumbled to life, making me aware of how powerful my motorcycle was. I could never live without Destiny or the motorcycle club.

He shook his head, spinning around and going to the building where he was going to have his classes. I couldn't wait until we met up again, which I knew was going to happen very soon. Tomorrow, I reminded myself. Tomorrow we were going to meet up again and it was going to be amazing.

Tomorrow was when the Valentine's Day party was going to happen.

Thinking about it, I couldn't help but groan. Even though I wanted to spend as much time with Nefion as possible, there was no denying that the Valentine party was the kind of event I didn't want to spend any time at. It was too well-mannered, too rich, and too extravagant.

But since I couldn't change anything about that, I had to go there.

I stepped onto the pedal, taking off on my motorcycle as I went back to the motorcycle club. Over there, I was going to meet up with the president and pretty much everyone else associated with the club. One of my dreams was to convince Nefion that he should join the club. I knew it would never happen, but maybe one day it could.

I sighed, pulling over when I was by the side of the club. As soon as I was there, I fished out my phone and loaded up a certain app I didn't like using, but which was very much necessary nowadays. If I wanted to stay in touch with Nefion, then I didn't have another choice.

He didn't post anything new on his profile, but I went there anyway to check out his photos. He was just so cute! A little younger than me, but certainly the right person for me.

It wasn't that I was jealous, but there was this guy that also had a crush on him, and I would do anything to fight him off. The problem was that we, the wolf bikers, already had a pretty bad reputation, following recent events between us and the bear bikers.

I heard the door opening and it was the president that was walking out. Striding out, I knew that something was up and that he needed my help with it. The only problem with that was that I didn't want anything major happening in my life right now.

The marriage thing and pretty much everything else that accompanied it was already turning my mind upside down. I had so many things to prepare for and Nefion didn't want to be involved in any of them.

CHAPTER 3

It was Valentine's Day and even though I knew I was supposed to be excited about it, I wasn't. I was standing somewhere in the room, holding a glass of water in my hand. Because I wasn't even 21 yet, everyone said that I couldn't drink anything alcoholic, which was bullshit. I couldn't wait until I was a little older so that I could drink anything I wanted.

Meanwhile, all of my friends were busy with other things and with themselves. They were dancing, chatting, and laughing quite loudly, the music reverberating in the room.

This Valentine's Day party was supposed to be a lead-up event before my wedding, but nobody in here cared about me. Not even my parents. They were on the other side of the room, chatting and kissing and generally having a lot of fun, which was something I couldn't have.

And the problem wasn't even with me. I wasn't antisocial or introspective or anything of the sort. I was just like everyone else. But I was realizing that my friends weren't really my friends.

They were always worried about themselves and no one else. When they wanted to hang out with me was when they remembered I existed.

I finished my drink and went over to the bathroom, stumbling on something warm and heavy. I almost lost my balance and fell over on my ass, but a strong hand grabbed my arm and held me in place. Shifting my eyes up, I realized that that person was none other than Cynem, who was regarding me with kind eyes.

His grip wasn't too strong and I could feel the confidence with which he was holding me. Our eyes met and I instantly felt a little confused about my feelings. There was no denying that he was hot, but was that really the only thing I felt for him?

I didn't know, but he was my only shot at turning the tables. I wanted to make this party better than it was, even though that was going to be very difficult. When they chose the music for the party, they didn't think it through.

They chose some of the worst music.

He let go of my arm before rubbing the back of his head. "Sorry about that. I meant to warn you before, but I didn't have enough time."

Now that he was filling my vision, I couldn't help but feel I had even forgotten about Palio. He was supposed to be somewhere at the party, but I couldn't see him. Maybe he finally realized that I didn't want to have anything to do with him…

It didn't matter how much he tried to make me understand I was his fated mate, I would never believe him. That was a promise I was making to myself.

And it wasn't like I could smell his scent at the party. It was strong and certainly very distinctive, but there were far too many people in the room. I couldn't even smell the scent of the guy that was in front of me and that was saying something, considering how intense it was.

I tried to smile, saying, "It's okay. I know it wasn't your fault."

He kept looking at me for what felt like an eternity, making me wonder what was going on in his mind. When I opened and closed my mouth, he said, "Do you wanna go outside with me? I don't mean to insult, but this party is trash. You deserve something better, like this bottle of wine."

As soon as he finished saying that, he produced a bottle of

wine, lifting it in his hand. I didn't know anything about wines, but the bottle looked pretty cool. A touch on it and I could tell that it was pretty cold, too. Licking my lips, I couldn't help but feel like going outside with him to empty it.

I checked around us, noticing that no one was looking at us. It was one of the benefits of people not giving a damn about me, I thought. It didn't even make sense. They came to this party because of me. There was even a huge neon sign hanging from one of the walls, mentioning my name and Palio's.

I didn't know what was going on in their minds, but I had enough of them and this party. Thinking that, the first thing that popped up in my mind was, "I don't want to spend a second longer here."

He widened his smile, turning around when I felt a scent in the air, and I couldn't overlook it. The first thought that came into my mind was that this couldn't be happening. The first time that I was finally letting loose and was ready to take the first step with Cynem, HE was going to show up.

I turned around again, finding Palio standing right behind me. He looked different, unlike his normal biker self. He had a suit on with a red tie, something that I thought not even in a million years would happen. He was even holding a single red rose in his hand, which was also just as mind-boggling. Him being the tough biker he was, I couldn't believe he ever would look more... refined.

He even got a haircut and did his beard before coming. Palio still stood out, but nobody could say that he wasn't giving his all.

His eyes were trembling slightly, showing me that something terrible was happening, and I didn't want to think about it. I wanted to pretend that this wasn't happening. It couldn't end well at all.

I could see his eyes changing, becoming more wolflike.

I tried to stand between the two of them, but Cynem pushed me aside. He didn't do it to hurt me, but because he had a score to settle with Palio. The two were about the same height and stature, making me wonder who would win in a fight. Palio was older and more experienced, which should give him an edge.

"You shouldn't be here," Palio growled, stepping toward his nemesis.

"Why not? You left your fiancé unattended and I was going to keep him company, something that you are obviously not fit for."

"You don't know anything about me," Palio argued, shoving Cynem gently. He wasn't trying to start a fight. He only shoved Cynem because he wanted to make his point clear. Either Cynem left us or something bad would happen.

"I know a lot about you. I know you are a wolf biker and that you shouldn't even be trying to marry someone so much younger than you. You got it in your head that you are his fated mate, which couldn't be any further from the truth. I don't believe in that sort of bullshit, which is why I'm telling you this – leave him alone before I make you regret it."

Blood was rushing to my head, making me feel tenser. This didn't look good at all. Everyone around us was still dancing and chatting, not even realizing the weight of what was happening. They were both alphas. They were so strong that a fight in here would destroy the party and it would mar my wedding, which wasn't something I wanted. I didn't want the wedding to happen, but not this way.

I stepped to stand between the two of them, turning my head from side to side.

"Hey, the two of you. Stop fighting. I don't like it when you fight."

Cynem looked down, finding my eyes. I thought he was going to object, but then he said, "Fine, but I'm only doing this for you. You don't want a fight to break out at the party and it won't. I promise you that."

After saying that, he turned around and left, leaving me wondering what was going on in his head. Did he still have such a strong crush on me? I didn't know, but everything was pointing toward that being the case, which was puzzling.

I was confused about my feelings toward him, which couldn't be good. After all, I was going to get married to someone else, who was less than pleased about having competition.

I turned again, looking right into Palio's eyes. He was shifting back to his normal self. His eyes went back to normal, which was very relieving.

"Why the hell did you say those things to him?" I asked, putting my hands on my waist. "He's a good person. He knows the limits and that he can't have me. I don't like you much, but since my father is forcing me to marry you, I'll have to."

He shook his head, saying, "You don't understand anything."

And as he finished saying that, I couldn't help but wonder why he did. What was it about us that I didn't understand?

CHAPTER 4

Palio

Cynem couldn't touch a follicle of his hair and I wasn't going to allow him. I would never. Nefion was mine. He was going to be my husband soon and I couldn't wait until I was putting the marriage ring on his finger, kissing his lips in front of everyone in the church.

I put my hand on his shoulder, leading him out of the party. He peeked over his shoulder, saying, "Hey, where the hell do you think you're taking me?"

"Out of here, for starters. Nothing good will come out of this party. Not to mention that I don't feel comfortable here anyway."

I thought he was going to object, but he was coming along as everyone kept ignoring us. As usual, they came to this party for themselves and no one else. I needed to keep that in mind.

"At least that's something we can agree on," he joked, opening the exit door and stepping out with me. We were in an alleyway between two buildings, happy that the pounding music wasn't shattering our eardrums anymore.

"Gosh, I feel like I can finally breathe again," he added, turning around and giving me the right opportunity to give him something else that I had with me. It was in the pocket of my pants. It was pretty small and was supposed to accompany the rose I had in my other hand.

I fished it out, moving my arm around him and showing him the rose first. He didn't mind that I was behind him and touching him, which was perfect. One of the reasons I was doing this was a pretty simple one. I needed to win his heart over.

I was pretty sure that doing that was going to be easy. After all, he was my fated mate, but I still needed to put the effort in. That's what this was all about. Not to mention that I loved him now that I knew he was my fated mate.

Nefion looked down, finding the rose in my hand. He picked it up slowly, saying, "It looks beautiful. I never thought that a biker like you actually had an eye for this kind of thing."

"Still thinking that I'm only a brute and don't know how to show niceness sometimes?" I asked, not feeling insulted by that. I knew the reputation that preceded wolf bikers like me. Everyone thought that we were just criminals. It wasn't like that at all. We were different, tougher, a little more ruthless than normal, but we were still people like everyone else.

"Something like that," he said, chuckling gently. "You got it just for me?"

"Yup," I responded, leaning in and smelling his scent through his perfume. It didn't matter how much perfume he sprayed on himself, his scent was always going to be strong and I was always going to know what it was like. There was no denying that.

I could already imagine our lives being like this for years on end, which was something I was looking forward to.

I moved my other arm so that my hand was showing him the other gift I bought. It was an engraved necklace, which made his eyes sparkle as soon as he noticed them. For a moment, he didn't know what to say.

"I also got this for you. It's supposed to make you remember me, wherever you are."

This was all happening because even though Nefion always pretended that he hated me, I knew he thought differently. I knew that he liked me, deep down there in his heart. It was just going to take him a while until he let that part of him out.

I shifted so that I was putting the necklace around his neck, and then I moved closer, pressing my body against his again. I was finding it very hard not to have an erection right now, which I was pretty sure he appreciated. He was the kind of guy that didn't like it when someone was being forceful to him.

And I wasn't going to be. I wanted to win his heart over and not force him to like me. Or at least, to force him to show me the true feelings he felt about us.

"It's really beautiful. It's even more beautiful than the rose, which is something I didn't think possible."

At this moment, I had already forgotten about Cynem and his attempts to steal my lover's heart. I thought that Nefion had already made it pretty clear that he wasn't interested.

I pondered kissing his cheek, but decided not to. Even though we kissed that time in front of his college, things were different now. I wanted him to take the other steps to building our relationship. I wanted him to be more proactive.

I moved away from him, happy when he said, "You've impressed me more than I thought you ever could."

"What can I say?" I said, smiling broadly. "I'm always like that. I'm always obsessed with you, and I just want to see you happy."

He took some steps toward me, putting his hands on my waist. His eyes were locked with me and what I did next felt natural. I put my hands on his jaws, pulled his head up, and then sealed our lips again. It was just like that time. His lips were very sweet and our kiss was extremely passionate.

There was no denying that he was falling more and more in love with me.

The kiss was so good that I closed my eyes and didn't think of anything in particular, just focusing on how much I wanted it to mean a lot more than it did.

He pulled his head back, regarding me with passionate eyes.

"I don't like you much, but if there's something you are good at, it's kissing," he purred, still not moving his hands away. I thought he was going to. It would be just like him to do something like that when it looked like things were going in my favor.

I put my arm around his shoulders and then started walking with him toward the parking space by the building. I didn't even worry that someone would come out looking for us. They most likely weren't going to.

"Where are you taking me this time?" He quizzed, not trying to move away from me. He was indeed coming with me. Nefion was curious and wanted to find out what I was thinking.

We rounded the corner of the building, finding the parking space and my motorcycle. Destiny was parked on one of the spots, just idling there. It looked pretty beautiful, especially under the gentle moonlight.

"I'm going to take you to a breathtaking spot. You deserve something a lot better than this shitty party."

He craned his head to look at me, saying, "I like the sound of that."

I sat on my motorcycle, put him on the backseat, and then revved up the engine. We took off moments later, the wind blowing against our faces. We didn't even look back to see if any of the partygoers had come out searching for us. They hadn't.

I took him through the streets and neighborhoods, stopping when we reached a hill. It overlooked the city and was the perfect spot for this special day that preceded our marriage.

I parked the motorcycle and he got off of it, stepping toward the edge of the hill. He was overlooking the city, eyes sparkling. I approached him from behind before I said, "You've never been here, have you?"

He shook his head gently.

"It's so beautiful. I didn't think a place like this existed."

"There's a lot about the city you don't know. Thankfully, now you finally have someone who can teach you everything about it."

I wrapped my arms around his lower torso, bringing him

closer to me. He didn't object, and I knew, from the start, he wasn't going to. I could feel his scent, his perfume, and the warmth of his body.

I could just imagine taking him to my bed, which I imagined he was also thinking about right now. But I wasn't going to. This was Valentine's Day, but we weren't boyfriends. It was a pity that we weren't, but there was nothing I could do about it.

"Maybe you aren't so bad after all," he purred, kissing me again and making me happy that we were. I could just imagine what our wedding was going to look like. I could imagine all the flowers that were going to decorate the church, the people inside it, the song that was going to play when he was coming toward me, and pretty much everything else my mind could conjure at the moment.

I wanted to make all of that happen and I couldn't wait until it was.

CHAPTER 5

Nefion

My heart was tight, but after everything he showed me, I thought that I could make this work. I was getting wedded, but it didn't mean that I was going to have to live with Palio for the rest of my life, right? I was going to get to know him better, which I knew was supposed to happen before the wedding, but here I was.

I shook my head at the thought, feeling my father's arm around mine. We were outside the church, just waiting for the right moment to step in. Someone inside the church was going to signal for us to walk in, and I was anxious about that.

I could see my future husband waiting for me on the other end of the room, with his hands crossed over his crotch. He was looking so professional and unlike his normal self, which was interesting.

He could be anyone he wanted, but he decided to become a biker. That was one question I needed to ask him when we were living alone in his house.

He wasn't rich, but he managed to finance his house. It wasn't very big. It didn't have everything I wanted, but it was better than nothing. Certainly a lot better than living in my parents' house, which was already very relieving. Just thinking that I wasn't going to have to go there after the wedding was already bringing a smile to my face.

I turned my head to look at my father, who was staring ahead with focused eyes. I had no idea what was going on in his mind and I wanted to probe it.

"Dad, do you really believe in all that fated mates bullshit?" I asked, knowing that I was probably crossing a line. It was better asking now when I still had time for that, I concluded. After the wedding, I didn't know when we would see each other again.

He turned his head to look at me, narrowing his eyes slightly.

"What kind of question is that? Do you even know what Palio went through to find out if we were right?"

I bit my bottom lip, realizing that, this whole time, I never bothered to ask them about it. I was so focused on college and graduating that I didn't even remember to do something as simple as that.

"That you were right?" I asked, feeling a little confused about that. I thought that he said they were going to find out who his partner was. "Do you mean that you already knew I was supposed to be his fated mate?"

It took him a while to respond, which was only making this more confusing to me. I didn't want to think that it was a red flag, but it looked like it was. I was a little terrified, but I wasn't going to back off on the wedding. I was going to go through with it.

After all, we already spent so much money and effort on making sure that everything was going to be right. Even my outfit was one of the most expensive things I had ever seen in my life.

"We suspected you might be. We were going to confirm it using the Sphere of Revelations, but you know what happened to it. It was shattered during an attack. I hate those Bear Bikers so much I want to see all of them dead. One day, they will pay for everything they did."

He was spitting saliva out of his mouth, making me feel the rage that was bubbling in his veins. If it was up to him, he would do a lot worse than that. I had never seen my father so angry before.

He was my Alpha father. My Omega father was inside the church, seated on one of the front benches. He was looking over his shoulder at us and wondering when we were going to be allowed in.

I turned my head to look back inside the room, just waiting for the song to kick in. When I breathed in and thought that it was still going to take a while until that happened, that's when it did.

I saw someone inside the church signaling for us to walk in, which we did. We crossed the front entrance and were soon walking down the aisle, everyone standing up and clapping.

It didn't matter how much I thought everything was wrong about the wedding. Now that it was finally happening and everything inside the main chamber looked so bright and beautiful, I couldn't imagine myself doing anything different.

I checked pretty much everyone that was in the chamber, clapping so loudly I couldn't hear anything else. Everyone that I knew from college was here, which was very exciting.

I could already see it happening. I could already imagine them talking about the wedding online for days on end. We lived in a medium-sized city, which meant that the marriage was a very important event, but wasn't the most striking one.

My father halted with me when we were in front of my husband. He took his arm off of me and then shook my future husband's hand, opening a big, bright smile. Unlike so many people in the city, he had no problem marrying me to a biker. He was actually okay with it.

After they shook their hands, my father went to one of the benches. It was where my Omega father was seated. When he was seated by his side, they held her hands together and waited for the continuation of the wedding.

I turned slowly, finding my future husband's eyes. They were full of love for me and how much he wanted me to be happy. It was great that he was feeling that way about it, but I couldn't shake off the feeling that something tiny was wrong about this. It was almost imperceptible, but I couldn't stop thinking about it.

And it was pointless to try and figure out what it was. I didn't think I could do that.

I sighed, trying to feel a tiny little happier about this than I was, just so that I could shake that feeling off and focus on the good aspects of getting wedded. It meant that I was going to live a different life and cease feeling like a teenager, which wasn't good.

I took a glance around the chamber, not finding someone that popped up in my mind all of a sudden. Palio could never know that the thought was in my mind right now. Cynem and his charming presence. I was pretty sure that news of the wedding was affecting him greatly and I couldn't do anything about that.

I knew that he liked me, but I thought that he'd already have shaken it off and focused on better things. After all, he'd already dated many Omegas. Was I really someone so dear to him? I didn't know but, either way, I'd like to make it so I wasn't saddening him.

I sighed, the priest reciting words from a book. A sudden thought popped up in my mind. I thought that bikers were supposed to marry their loved ones on the road. I'd seen documentaries about it. Bikers usually got wedded while riding on their motorcycles and not in churches.

Palio was different from his kin, and I couldn't help but wonder why. I supposed that he was doing this to please my father, who didn't have anything to do with any motorcycle club.

His MC buddies weren't here either, which only sprouted more questions in my mind. I didn't know what was going on, but it was difficult to focus on anything else when my future husband was already putting the marriage ring on my finger.

Then, I did the same for him. He cupped my face with his firm hands and we kissed, everyone clapping after the priest said we were husband… and husband. I chuckled at the thought, at the moment focusing on just one thing – how sweet and needy his kiss was.

It was like he was releasing everything he'd been obsessing over this whole time. He was kissing me with delight, only pulling his head back when he had his fill.

I was breathless, my lungs expanding and contracting. There was something different about that kiss I couldn't put my finger on. Even though I couldn't tell what he was thinking about right now, I could say that our wedding night was going to happen one way or another. And Palio being a biker, I couldn't help but wonder if he was going to do something different from what most people normally would.

"Time to go, love," he said, taking my hand and leading me down the aisle again. We stepped out of the church and everyone gathered around us, throwing rice over our heads. We ducked and climbed up his motorcycle. Nobody was going to follow us, which was something I was happy about.

We finally had privacy and the world was ours to tackle.

CHAPTER 6

Palio

I was happy beyond anything I had ever felt before, standing behind the door to our room. I got a house just for us, which I knew he was happy about. I wrapped my fingers around the doorknob and then twisted it, opening the door.

Our room was very simple, but it was enough. Nefion was already taking off his clothes. He looked so pretty and inviting. He had his earbuds on, which meant he couldn't hear that I was walking in.

I closed the door gently behind me, stepping toward him before wrapping my arms around his torso. I kissed the nape of his neck and then took off his earbuds, loving the way his warmth was pulsing out of his body.

"You look so lovely, dear," I murmured, peppering the side of his neck again and again. We were fated mates and there was no doubt about that. When I was by his side, I couldn't think about anything else. All I could think about was how much I loved him and how much I wanted to spend as much time with him as possible.

"You caught me off guard."

"Does that bother you?" I asked, helping him unbutton his shirt. I was finally feeling it. His bare, exposed skin, and it was different from everything I had felt before. It was so warm and smooth, unlike my body. He was going to feel it too when I took off my clothes, I thought, purring against his neck.

"Not at all," he replied, taking off his shirt and melting in my arms. I moved my hands over his shoulders, massaging him. I loved how smooth and soft his skin was, and I couldn't help but pepper it with several more kisses.

He squirmed, grinding his body against me as his ass rubbed against my crotch. Gosh, he was turning me on so much I was already getting an erection. I was already thinking about throwing his legs open and burying my cock inside of him, which I was very sure he wanted as well.

I brushed my finger over his lips, turning him around slowly before I sealed my lips to his again. He melted in my arms again, held in place by them. If it wasn't for them, he would be falling on the floor.

I dug my tongue into his mouth, battling against his tongue for what felt like an eternity. Nefion was an Omega who wanted me to knock him up, but he was also braver than most other Omegas. He could stand up for himself, which was very unlike his kind.

His lips brushing against me, I couldn't help but push him against the wall, though I did so gently. I didn't want to hurt him and I never would. Not to mention that I would never forgive myself if something like that happened.

My dick was just so hard and I couldn't wait until I was knotting him. I was pretty sure that the same thought was swirling around in his mind, too.

Moments later, I pulled my head back and I noticed that he was breathless. He was trying to breathe, but he was having difficulty doing so. I let a couple of moments pass and when I noticed that he was already feeling better, I got on my knees and started to unbuckle his belt.

I looked up, noticing that his lips were parted. He nodded and I went ahead, happy that I got my confirmation. I took off his belt and his pants fell to the floor, finally revealing my prize. I loved how big his bulge was and that his cock was already hard. I could even see a stain of pre-come on the fabric.

No denying it. I was going to knot him on our wedding night, already building toward having one of the best families in the world. Even though it was going to be difficult and a little weird, it was also going to be great.

I'd also have to come clear to the president and tell him that I wasn't going to be a part of the club anymore, but that was okay. I was pretty sure he was going to understand it.

His scent was stronger now than it had ever been, impregnating my lungs. I basked myself in it and then started to lower his pair of briefs, which made him a little uncomfortable. I thought he was going to ask me to stop and take things a little slower, but he didn't.

He was going to lose his virginity and there was nothing he could do to stop it. I mean, there was, but he was already too invested in it to ask me to stop now.

I finished pulling his pair of briefs down, loving the way his cock came jumping out. It was bouncing up and down, pre-come seeping out of the slit. I grabbed it and lowered my head, sticking my tongue out. I brushed it over the tip of his cockhead, finally getting a taste of his release.

He groaned, closing his eyes. With the help of my other hand, I took him to the bed, where he sat. He was in the perfect position for what I was looking for to do with him. I gave his cock a couple of strokes, making sure that I was giving him as much pleasure as possible.

My heart was pounding in my chest, which was something that didn't happen often, even when I was having sex with another guy.

I looked up, noticing that his eyes were still closed. Opening a dirty smile, I dove down and wrapped my lips around his shaft. I worked first on the cockhead, loving the shape of it. His body was trembling, pleasure all over it.

Nefion was feeling so much lust I was already wondering what he was going to feel like when I was inside of him. Moments later, I lowered my head as I put more of his shaft inside my mouth.

Playing with his balls, I thought he was going to come when his dick started to spasm between my lips, but it was just a false flag.

"Knot me," he purred, making me widen my smile. There was nothing better than hearing that coming from my love.

"With pleasure," I said, getting off his cock and laying him down on the bed. I turned him around, took off my clothes, and started to stroke my cock. My shaft was already hard. Nefion was so wet right now I knew I could breach him without lube. Thinking that, I smiled again as I climbed up the bed and grabbed him by his waist.

He gripped the bedsheets tightly when I nudged his orifice with my cock. I was just playing with him in the beginning, wondering how he was feeling about this. His body was covered in sweat, and it looked like he was ready. And as long as he was ready, so was I.

I stayed still for a couple of moments, wondering what was going on in his mind right now.

I pushed myself into his orifice as I breached it, going all the way to the bottom. Rolling my hips, I started to pound in and out of him, loving the way we were becoming one. My dick grew bigger than it had ever been and I knew that now I'd only get out of him after I knotted him. He was moaning and groaning, pleasure spreading all over his body.

I increased my pace when I felt more comfortable inside of him. I kicked it up a notch when I was even more comfortable with how things were happening. He started to match me thrust for thrust, which made our sex even better.

Nefion felt so small underneath me and if there was one other thing I was thinking about right now, it was how much I needed to protect him from everything and anyone that wanted to harm him.

And then I came inside of him, knowing that I was knocking him up and that there was no turning back. Now that I was inside of him, I knew he was going to have my baby. I wasn't going to stop with just one baby, though.

When my dick stopped throbbing inside of him, I pulled out and fell down onto the bed. Wrapping my arms around him, I snuggled him between them and we fell asleep.

I couldn't wait until I found out what the days ahead had in store for us.

CHAPTER 7

Nefion

What happened that night was amazing and I'd never forget it. After a hot shower, Palio was already opening the door of the bathroom and wrapping his arms around me. He caught me off guard again, which was something that wasn't supposed to happen.

I didn't know what was up with my nose, but I should have noticed him coming, especially now that my mind was used to the fact that he was my husband.

The badass biker was my husband. We were living in a very small house, but it all still felt so odd. He shouldn't be looking to settle down with anyone. Looking up and at his eyes, though, I couldn't help but realize that his love for me was genuine. I just kind of wished he wasn't so obsessed with me all the time. I was pretty sure that one of these days I'd snap, shouting at his face that he wasn't supposed to catch me off guard so often.

Right now, though, it was the day after the wedding and I couldn't think of those things. I just let his firm arms melt me in them, his lips going for the nape of my neck and pecking it. I melted in his embrace once more and could see the same happening in all the days that were going to follow this one.

Even though I was married, I wasn't sure about the whole 'fated mates' thing. I supposed I needed to get to know him better before even considering anything along the lines of a divorce, though.

"You look so lovely this morning," he purred, looking at my reflection in the mirror. He was naked, as was I. His dick was already hard, making me think that he was planning on knotting me again soon. While I wanted that, I was pretty sure that he had his own things to take care of.

Not to mention that I was planning on going to the library for studies. There were so many things I needed to read and assimilate. My degree was a very difficult one and I was pretty sure he was well aware of that.

I pecked his lips, saying, "And you look just as lovely. I didn't think that getting married was going to change my life so much."

"It's only the beginning," he said, moving his hand over my belly and making me remember that something ground-breaking happened the other night. I was so worried about some other things that the thought didn't cross my mind until it was already too late. He really knotted me. I mean, I guess that the thought must have popped up sometime in my mind, but I must have brushed it off. I didn't think that this biker was so in love with me that he wanted me to have his baby.

My breathing quickened. It was one thing not thinking something and another letting something like that happen. I should've been more cautious, even though I supposed that, now, it was too late and I couldn't do anything about it. Short of getting an abortion, which I didn't think I could, there was no viable alternative. I didn't want to feel that I was killing a life. That was a thought that always popped up in my mind when the word 'abortion' was brought up.

"Something wrong?" He asked, stopping the movement of his hand around my belly.

"No. Don't worry about it. I was just concerned with my midterm - the one that I'll have tomorrow morning. I need to be ready for it. You know how important getting my degree is."

He softened his expression now that he realized it wasn't anything he should be worried about. He moved his hand down, grabbing my balls and giving them a little squeeze. I closed my eyes, letting waves of pleasure move through my body. It was difficult to think that anything was wrong with our life when he was already making me feel this way.

He pulled his hand back, keeping his body pushing against me. He was just hugging me from behind, feeling the warmth of my body.

But the thing about growing a life inside my belly was true. I didn't know if I wanted it or even if I was ready for it. Not to mention that I didn't think I would have time to care for a baby.

Moments later, Palio stepped away from me and went back into the room, where he put on his clothes. After he finished adjusting his leather jacket with the insignia of his motorcycle club, he said, "I need to go see the president. He's waiting for me."

Looking at him through the reflection in the mirror as I did my hair, I asked, "To do what?"

"I can't be your husband, the father of our little one, and a biker at the same time. I know it's a difficult decision and I pondered once about convincing you to join the club, but I couldn't. My mind is made up."

I blinked twice, finding that surprising. Never thought that Palio would consider inviting me into the club. Now that he mentioned that, I was thinking that it would be pretty cool, though only for a day.

I would do it just to see what being a biker was like from their point of view. It wasn't like I would suddenly decide that becoming a biker was what I wanted. After all, there was nothing worse than contradicting myself. I had always hated bikers and that would never change, even though Palio was changing a lot about the way I looked at them.

He came to me and gave me one last kiss, saying, "I'll be back soon. It should take me only a couple of hours to go through the process. I'm pretty sure that the president will think I'm betraying him. After all, he likes me a lot. It will be fine, though. He'll realize that he can't keep me there forever."

I checked his expression, realizing that he was speaking the truth.

I put the comb down on the sink before saying, "If you say so, but if anything happens, don't hesitate to call my father. He'd be happy to help you. Not to mention that he's probably looking for a bodyguard. You could work for him."

He smiled without showing his teeth, and even though he was trying to show that he was comfortable about this, I could tell that he wasn't. I didn't know what was about it, but it looked like he wasn't keen on the idea of working for my father.

He kissed me again before going out and climbed up on his bike, riding away. I was outside the house, looking at him as he went and turned left. When he was out of sight, I turned back around before noticing that someone was coming in my direction.

The first thought that popped up in my mind was that it was a criminal trying to rob me, but after turning again and checking out who it was, I was surprised when I realized it was none other than Cynem.

I didn't think he was going to show up all of a sudden. The fact that he did rang some alarms in my mind. What if he had been waiting outside until I wasn't with my husband anymore?

I didn't know, but I was still cautious.

His feet halted in front of me as he opened a smile. "Nefion, I'm so sorry about it. I meant to come to the wedding, but I couldn't. I was caught up in something."

I blinked twice, happy that he was mentioning the wedding and the fact that he hadn't been in it.

"It's okay. You're here now and that's what matters."

That's what I said, but I still wanted to punch his face so hard that he wasn't at the wedding. I didn't know what was about it, but I wanted his approval as well. I wanted things to be okay between us, and I was pretty sure that he thought the same way. After all, even though we had once tried to be lovers, it didn't have to mean we couldn't be friends.

A moment of silence ensued and I wondered what he was thinking about. He looked up, finding my eyes and when I was going to open my mouth to invite him in, he grabbed my face and kissed me.

I pushed him away from me, stumbling back into my house. I narrowed my eyes as I blushed.

"What was that?" I barked, not liking that he was leering at me.

He approached me, looking very much determined about what he was doing.

"I came here for you. I miss you so much, and there's something about Palio you need to know."

CHAPTER 8

I shook my head, stepping farther into my house as I tried to shut the door. But he put his hand against it, preventing me from doing that. Seconds later, he was stepping into my house as well, and then he closed the door behind him. I had no idea what was going on in his mind, but I wasn't interested.

My hand went for my phone, I fished it out of my pocket, and when I tried to call the police, he snatched it from me and put it on a side table. He was trying to show me that he came here in peace, but I knew better. As far as I was concerned, he invaded my house and needed to be kicked out of it as soon as possible.

"Cynem, you're going to regret this," I warned, going to the kitchen and grabbing a knife. Pointing it against him, I did everything in my power to show him that I wasn't kidding. If he tried anything similar to what he did, I wouldn't be opposed to hurting him.

He stepped toward me, grabbed my wrist, and lowered it as I realized I didn't have enough strength to fight him. Not to mention that he was an Alpha, much stronger than me, and also a wolf shifter.

I could see it in his eyes, the way that they were changing and becoming more wolflike. His fur was beginning to show as well, which wasn't good news. I didn't want him to transform. Unlike

Palio, he couldn't control that other side of him.

I put the knife back down by the side of the sink as he locked his eyes with me again.

"I know I lost you, but maybe not all hope is lost."

And after a moment of silence, he asked, "He knocked you up, didn't he?"

I waited to see if he was going to do anything else. When I realized that he wasn't going to back off, I responded, "I don't think that's something you need to know anything about. It's none of your business."

He shook his head. "I'm just trying to help you. How much do you think you know about Palio?"

"That he's a much better person than you."

"If that's the way you think of it, then I'm disappointed in you. You used to be much more of a fighter."

I tipped up my chin. Even though he was an Alpha and I was just an Omega, he wasn't going to change my mind about the wedding. I was looking forward to the life I was going to have with my husband, which was a lot more than anything else I ever had in my life.

"I'm still the same person. It's you who changed. You'd never have kissed me the way you did."

"You don't know anything about me," he affirmed, growling and grabbing my face with his hand, digging his fingers into my skin. I felt powerless. It was his power over me that was making me do nothing. I tried to fight against him, but it was impossible.

"You are hurting me."

As soon as I said that, he pulled his hand back and stepped away from me. I fell on my knees on the floor, panting. I never thought that the guy who was my crush would do what he did. He was ruthless, his body changing still.

"I know that Palio is ditching the gang. I'll join them and replace him."

I looked up, finding him with his back turned to me. I could see tears forming in his shirt and pants, signaling his ongoing transformation. I had no idea what was going on in his mind, but it was scaring me. I didn't have my phone with me. I wanted to call the police before he hurt me again.

"What?" I asked, finding his affirmation hard to grasp. "I know he's going to do that, but what do you have to do with it? It has no relation to you."

He turned around slowly, his eyes holding me as though he was pondering if he should eat me alive. I was so scared that my skin was cold. My heart was so tight I thought I was going to have a heart attack.

"I'm going to replace him. I'm going to take his place, become the next sergeant at arms, and then I'll kill him. I can never forgive him for what he did."

I stood up slowly, supporting my weight against the wall.

"And what did he do against you?"

"There's something you need to know. You remember that I came from the Land of Nanape, don't you?" Just as he finished saying that, he stepped toward me and when I thought he was going to hit me, his expression softened up.

I remembered what happened in Nanape. The kind of things that happened there, the war, and the number of people who died in their land... I could never forget that. It had been all over the news. I usually was the kind of person who tried to understand other people's points of view, so it wasn't surprising that the war shook me to the core.

"I can never forget what happened in Nanape, but what does it have to do with anything we are discussing?" I asked, feeling breathless.

"It feels as though everything was staged, but it wasn't. You didn't know that Palio was in the war, fighting for our country. You don't know the kind of things he did. There's a reason why he is a Wolf Biker. He killed so many people, my parents included. I found out about it not too long ago. You don't know how long I've been looking for the truth."

I blinked slowly, stepping away from him. Putting as much distance as possible between us was necessary right now. He was huge, very imposing, and his presence alone was enough to make anyone turn their attention to him.

"I think you got it wrong. Palio was never in the war and he never killed anyone. He is not a criminal or a sadist."

He scoffed, pulling out his phone. He turned it so that I could see what the screen was showing me, smirking when he realized I understood he was right.

The video was showing everything, which was confusing and enlightening at the same time. Palio had indeed been in the war, unless this was some kind of well-made deep fake video. Knowing how well technology was advancing, that could be the case, but something in my heart was telling me it wasn't.

I now had several questions to ask Palio and I didn't know if I had the courage to do that.

"And how do you know he really was involved when your parents were killed?"

"I can't tell you that. I can't show you the document, but it says specifically that he was involved. He was part of the mission where they killed everyone in my city."

Studying his face, I could tell he wasn't lying about any of what he was saying. Nevertheless, whether he was truly saying the truth or not didn't matter. What mattered was that he was raging. He was so much more than angry. He wanted to rip open Palio's neck and that was putting it mildly.

I didn't think I'd ever seen someone so angry before.

"I can't let you do that. You used to be a better person than this," I lamented, walking past him and wondering if he was going to stop me. I picked up my phone as I studied what he was going to do. I thought he was going to lunge at me, but he held his ground for a couple of seconds. When he realized that I wasn't going to change my mind, he walked out of the house.

He halted, turning around to peek over his shoulder. He was looking at me when he said, "You should ditch him, too. He lied to you about his past, didn't he?"

I opened my mouth, but there was nothing that could be said. I knew he was right, even though it was just in part. Palio never lied about his past, but I also never asked him about it.

Satisfied with my lack of answer, Cynem turned left and started to walk away. When he was out of sight, I already felt much more relieved. I walked back into the house, sat on the floor, and started crying against my knees.

I couldn't believe that everything appeared to be spiraling out of control. I couldn't believe that someone already had it in for my husband, who was someone I was beginning to like.

I had no idea what was going to happen, but when he was back home, I needed to confront him about it.

CHAPTER 9

Palio

The president slammed his hand against the table, looking across it at me. "You have no right to be doing this. You're the most important citizen of the pack."

"I'm sorry, but it has to be done. I'm married now," I said, lifting my hand and showing him the marriage ring. He glanced at it, remembering that he'd been in the wedding and couldn't have done anything to stop it, even though he wanted to do so quite a lot.

"This is a mistake. You know that the Bear Bikers have it in for us. We need you to keep them at bay."

"I'm aware of that, but you'll be fine." I rounded the table, putting myself in front of him. After putting my hand on his shoulder, I affirmed, "Even without me, you'll be fine. I'm sure of it."

He ran his hand through his thick, bushy beard, sighing and stepping away from me. He was looking at the window when someone knocked on the door. "Boss, you have a visitor and he wants to talk to you."

The president turned around, looking at me with quizzing eyes. I shrugged and he shuffled over to the door, opening it. While the Wolf Bikers were a large group, he didn't try to make it look like a company. He didn't have a secretary or anything of the sort. For the most part, it was just him and the higher-ups running the show.

He tried to make everyone feel like we were part of a family and it was working. Everybody here was loyal to him, and I didn't think that that would ever change.

Whoever was on the other side of the door though… I couldn't help but wonder who he was.

"Who is it?" He asked, raising his voice. The environment inside the club was quite packed, music thudding through the walls most of the time. We always got some complaints from the police and the neighbors about that, but they couldn't do much. That was just how we were.

"His name is Cynem Zale. I don't know much about him, just that he's thinking about joining the club."

The president pulled at his beard, saying, "Let him in. I suppose there's no harm in talking."

The fact that he was looking pensive and knew Cynem's name was curious, to say the least. I thought that he didn't know who he was. It looked like I was wrong about that. Maybe Cynem was more important than he appeared to be, which was something that I didn't think I'd ever be saying.

He stepped into the room, smirking as his eyes changed slightly. I knew we didn't like each other much, but I didn't think that he loathed me. Something happened not too long ago and I couldn't put my finger on it.

The president checked him out from bottom to top, scoffing. "A college boy like you, and you think that you can join us? Go back to your mommy, kiddo. Your place isn't here."

"Sir, I'm willing to do anything and everything for the cause. I want to prove that I'm worthy."

The president studied him for a couple more seconds, saying, "Well, I suppose that we can at least try and see if you'd be accepted. I don't think you will, but there's no harm in trying, right, Chains?"

Chains was my nickname in the club. We often used our nicknames when referring to each other, though not all the time. I was still stupefied by what was happening to say anything. For the first few seconds after he made that question, I stayed silent.

Realizing that I was looking like a fool – and especially in front of someone that considered me his nemesis – I cleared my throat and replied, "Whatever you want to do, I'm okay with it. The club is yours, after all." After another moment of silence, I added, "So, are we good?"

The president shook his head, sighing. "We are, but only for the time being. I know you'll change your mind eventually."

I curled up the sides of my lips. I walked through the door, stepped outside the room, and said, "Maybe."

"I know you will," he argued.

I walked out of the club as everyone greeted me and I said the bad news. It didn't matter how much I wanted to downplay it – leaving the club where I spent most of my life was always going to hurt me.

Seconds later, I was back on my bike and looking behind me. The building where the club was located would always remain in my mind and I would always think of it fondly.

From now on, I wasn't a biker anymore. The first thing I did, which I never would in other cases, was to put on a helmet. It felt snug against my head, which was way more than I thought I would ever say about it.

I turned on the engine of the motorcycle and then drove home, impatient about being with my husband again. I was pretty sure that he was already feeling the same way, thinking about the life we were going to have together.

But I was going to be respectful of his schedule and that he needed to study. I just wanted to kiss him again and there was nothing wrong with that.

I parked inside the garage of our house, opened the door, and when I found him seated on the floor crying against his knees, I knew something was wrong.

I didn't know what it was, but my heart was tight and I was going to do everything in my power to get the truth out of him.

I got on one knee, grabbing his shoulders. I was shaking him gently when I asked, "Hey, what happened? Why are you crying?"

He was still crying even after I asked him that question, making me feel more worried about it. I thought he was going to keep ignoring me, but then he lifted his head, his eyes red.

"You lied to me."

I gave him an uncomfortable smile, not knowing where that came from. We just got married the day before. What was he going on about?

"What did I lie to you about?" I asked, hoping that he was going to spit out the answer and not dance around it.

"That you weren't in the war. I know you didn't say anything about it, but I think that's something we should all have known before my father decided to marry me to you."

"I married you because we were made for each other and not for another reason."

Seconds later, he was still staring at me, which was making me feel uncomfortable. Not only that, but he was also making me feel that this was unfair. I never thought that my background in the war was important.

It happened so long ago and I wasn't in the military anymore, of course. I wasn't even a biker any longer. I was a person like any other, trying to build a life with my husband.

"But is it true? That you were in the war?"

"Who told you about it?" I asked, helping him stand up. Now that our eyes were almost level, I could feel that I had better control of what was happening. Still, I didn't like where this was going.

"Cynem..." He replied after what felt like an eternity, making me feel as if he just punched me in the gut. I knew something was up when Cynem showed up all of a sudden at the club. I never thought he would. I thought he was just a college student like any other. "He told me everything. He came here after you left."

"I knew he was up to something," I grumbled, punching the air. "And now it looks like he's going to become a biker. He's going to become a member of the Wolf Bikers."

"He told me about that, too. He also told me something else. He said that you killed his parents, and he wants revenge."

I narrowed my eyes, finding that unbelievable. "I was in the war. I did horrible things for the government, but I never killed his parents. Even if by some miracle that happened, I couldn't have known. I doubt that they were innocent, anyway."

A moment of unnerving silence impregnated the room, making me feel that Nefion was going to say the unthinkable. Moments later, he threw his arms around me and hugged me tightly.

Seeing that, I put one arm around him and murmured into his ear, "I'm sorry about everything that happened, but I never killed his parents. I refuse to believe someone thinks I did that. I'm going to talk to him face-to-face when I can and I'll clear everything up. I promise you that."

Nefion looked up, finding my eyes.

"I trust you."

And having his trust was more important than pretty much everything else that happened today. It meant that our wedding was still in good standing and that I didn't lose his love.

Regardless, I felt like what we had between us already had a crack in it.

CHAPTER 10

Nefion

The room was dark and I couldn't stay inside of it much longer. The reason for that was pretty simple. I couldn't stay in my husband's house for another minute. Cynem managed to become a biker, and I didn't know how that even happened. All I knew was that he pulled it off and I kept thinking that something terrible was going to come out of that.

I tried contacting him, but he didn't want to pick up the calls. My phone was turned on and I couldn't stand the spread of misinformation and fake news anymore. It was flying from the mouth of one person and then reaching pretty much everyone in the city, and that was saying something, considering that it wasn't very small.

People were saying that Palio was a murderer and that he'd been lying about that this whole time. I couldn't keep going like this, thinking that everything would sort out in the end. It wasn't going to and Cynem was planning his attack.

He didn't tell anyone in the biker club, as else they'd already have kicked him out. But he was a capable man and he'd gather enough supporters to go up against Palio. I was certain about that and it was the only thought in my mind right now.

That and one more thing – the fact that the months were passing and my belly was growing huger. I didn't know if Palio was aware of what he did. I mean, he should be, right? I didn't know for sure, but he was still the same lovely guy from before.

I didn't tell my father the news, though I was pretty sure that, by now, he knew something was up.

I turned in the bed slowly, looking at him and realizing that someone like him didn't deserve what was coming for him. Still, I was scared. He worked as one of my father's bodyguards and he was amazing at his job. I couldn't be any prouder of him and, yet, I knew something was wrong.

Nothing worse than questioning myself all the time, though, I thought, pushing his arm off of me, slipping out of the bed, and walking to the bathroom without making much noise. The phone was turned off, put into silent mode, and it wouldn't wake Palio up. Thank goodness. I wouldn't be doing this without knowing that I was going to be okay.

The bathroom was right by the bedroom. I opened the door slowly, stepped inside of it, and lowered my PJ's pants. I had a pregnancy test tube with me. I didn't think I was going to need it per se, but it was still better than waiting and worrying that I might not be right after all.

I did what I had to do with the pregnancy test, shaking it in front of me as I waited for the results. It felt like minutes were passing, even though it was just seconds. The first red line appeared and then the second one, giving me the confirmation I was looking for. Or rather, the one I was trying to avoid.

It was true. I was pregnant with Palio's baby and I didn't know what to do.

As soon as I got the answer I was looking for, I tossed the tube into the toilet and flushed it. I was relieved that Palio would never find out about it, but it still didn't solve my problems.

I didn't know if I wanted to have the baby.

And the reason behind that was that I made a mistake when we had sex and he didn't use protection. The first days after it happened, I was lying to myself.

I kept saying that it wasn't going to happen, that I wasn't pregnant, and that I had a full life ahead of me without having to care for a baby. Now that I was thinking about it, I realized I'd been so stupid. Of course he knocked me up. That was just like him. He liked to lie and use me.

All because he ventured somewhere dangerous and life-threatening to find out if I was his fated mate. After all, every Alpha had an Omega, and apparently I was supposed to be his partner – for the rest of my life.

I was fine with that as long as our married life didn't have to involve anything more complicated than loving and having sex, but I knew he wanted more. It was clear in his eyes how he wanted to build a family with me. He wanted to have not just this baby, but many.

I didn't think I was ready for that, even though I also knew it was already too late. If I said to my Omega father what was going on in my mind, he would slap me around and say how stupid about it I was being. But for him, it had been so much easier. He didn't have to marry a biker, didn't have to choose between his life and having a family, and was able to better choose what he wanted when he was much older.

I opened the door of the bathroom slowly, with my PJ's pants back on, and walked to the outside of the house. When I was in the backyard, I walked over to the swing that we had. I sat on it, started to swing, and then made a call I thought I never would.

I needed help and there was only one person I knew that had been in the same situation I now was.

It was dark, but I knew he was going to look at the number and pick up the call as soon as he saw that it was me.

Minutes later, when I heard his voice, it was like I knew everything was going to be much better.

"Bren, it's so good to hear your voice. I'm so sorry I'm calling you in the middle of the night. It's just that… Something terrible is happening to me and I don't have anyone I can talk to."

"Nefion? Oh no, it's okay. You can talk about whatever it is that's bothering you."

I checked what was around me, feeling a little paranoid. I felt like Palio would jump out of the shadows and confront me about the call. Thankfully, it looked like that wasn't going to happen.

"I think I'm pregnant." I tsked, feeling impatient. "Scratch that. I *know* I'm pregnant and I don't think I'm ready for that. Can I stay at your place? It's the only place where I know I'll be safe until I can figure out what to do."

"Of course you can stay here for as long as you want, but what's really going on? You've always said that you were happy with Palio."

"I'm just scared. I don't want to have a baby."

"That's understandable, but you should have talked to him about it before it happened. Now, it might be a little late for that. How long has it already been since it happened?"

"I think… A couple of months. It's been difficult to keep track of time. I'm focused on college and figuring out my life. That's one of the reasons why I don't want my life to change so much. I want to develop my professional career and grow as a person."

"Do you think you can have all of that even though you would have to care for him?"

"I don't know. All I know is that I feel suffocated. I need time to think and a better place to stay."

I heard a deep, audible sigh coming from the other end of the call.

"That's okay. I know what you're going through. Just come to my house as soon as you can."

"Can it be tonight? I don't know if I can spend another day here. I know it will hurt him, but I plan on figuring out everything before it's too late. I'm such a stupid kid."

"You aren't a kid anymore and you need to grow up."

"You're right. Thank you for being my friend."

CHAPTER 11

Palio

I dropped my arm over the other side of the bed, hoping to find my mate, but it was empty. I didn't feel anything, didn't feel anyone, and my heart was soon pounding and racing. My eyes shot open. Something was wrong and I didn't know what it was. He was always by my side when I woke up.

The first thought that popped up in my mind was that he'd gone to the kitchen to make breakfast. I sat up on the bed, looking from side to side.

If that was the case, then the smell of bacon should already be floating in the air, but that wasn't what I was feeling right now. If anything, I couldn't smell anything and could feel like there was an emptiness in my heart.

I shoved the comforter over to the other side of the bed, jumped out, and rushed over to the kitchen. I was always obsessed and desperate when it came to Nefion.

It wasn't that I thought someone would try to harm him, but I was so deeply in love with him that I needed, all the time, to know where he was and what he was doing. I was just finding it so weird that he'd disappeared all of a sudden without telling me anything about it.

I went to the other rooms of the house, including the bath- room and the living room, but I didn't find him. I looked outside and noticed that my motorcycle was still on the driveway. He didn't take it to go anywhere, that much was certain.

Still, I couldn't help but feel that something happened at night, and I couldn't put my finger on it. I jumped back into the house, snatched my phone, and dialed his number. I thought that I was going to hear his phone ringing in the house, but it wasn't. It was calling him, but he wasn't picking it up.

I was more desperate now than I'd ever been in my life and that was saying something. I'd gone through so much.

"Fuck," I barked, hurling the phone against the wall and hearing the screen cracking. I didn't feel bad about that. The phone didn't matter right now. What mattered was finding out what happened to my Omega and why he wasn't in the house all of a sudden.

Could I think that maybe he went out to buy something? No, I didn't think so. Not only did we live in a neighborhood where we couldn't have commercial buildings nearby, he never went out without first telling me about it, and certainly not in the middle of the night.

No. Something was up and I needed to know what it was.

Just when I was crossing the living room, I heard the sound of a motorcycle pulling over. At first, I didn't think much of it. It could be anything. Maybe someone from the club was looking to make small talk with me or something like that. It wouldn't be the first time it happened.

Nevertheless, I needed to go to the window to find out what was going on.

I went there, opened it, and wasn't surprised when I saw Cynem getting off his bike. He took off his helmet and leered at me, a mischievous smile appearing on his face.

"Looks like I just found what I came here looking for," he growled, his voice getting thicker.

"I don't have time for you," I said, shutting the window and going to my bedroom. I put my clothes back on and even my biker jacket, which was an item that I hadn't used since getting out of the club. It made me feel calmer.

I had a plan. I was going to get on my motorcycle and go to the club. The president was still one of my friends and he would understand what was happening. He would offer his help, which was everything I needed.

The first suspicion I had over what happened was that someone had kidnapped Nefion. I didn't see any indications that that was the case, but it wasn't that he disappeared without telling me anything. I didn't see any signs that one of the doors or one of the windows was forced, but I wasn't going to wait until my mind figured out everything on its own.

All that mattered was that the possibility was there. I needed to clear that up before it was too late.

I was just crossing the doorway out of the bedroom when my eyes caught sight of something small and white on the side table. At first, I didn't think much of it. It was probably just a small piece of paper left by Nefion or me that we forgot about, but then I decided to take a closer look.

It was addressed to me, and my heart was already pounding harder again.

Since it was addressed to me, then most likely it was regarding his disappearance. My mind didn't even want to consider the possibility, but Nefion might have walked out on his own, which hurt me.

After all, even though we didn't have much money, I was still doing everything in my power to help him. I was always doing everything I could to show him how important our love was.

I picked up the small piece of paper, unfolding it as I started to read what it said.

My mind was so focused on it that it didn't even register that Cynem just kicked the front door open.

Hey, it's me, your beloved husband. I'm so sorry I have to write this letter to you, but I really don't see another way out of this. I'm leaving tonight. I'm not going to tell you where I'm going, but you need to know that you won't be seeing me for quite some time.

The thing is that... I'm pregnant and I'm sure that the baby is yours. It's all so overwhelming that I don't want to even think about it for now. I know I'm probably being unfair about the whole thing, but I just need to be with someone that was once in a very similar situation.

I need to think things through. I think... I really love you and I want to make our baby happy as well, but I need to understand what's really going on in my mind and how I feel about everything. My life is changing so much, which is something I never thought about when we were still planning the wedding.

Don't come looking for me. I'll be back when I'm ready, if you are okay with that.

Nefion

I was still holding the piece of paper in my hand, and my whole body was trembling. I couldn't believe that the worst nightmare of my life was happening right in front of my eyes. I put the piece of paper back down on the table and turned around when I felt something heavy hitting my face.

I fell over on my back, shooting my eyes open as I tried to piece together what just happened. And then I saw him. Cynem. He was a couple of feet across from me, looming in front of me.

"Where's Nefion?" He barked, his whole body changing. He was becoming more wolflike, and the look in his eyes told me that he was thinking of just one thing – having his revenge. He couldn't accept that Nefion married me instead.

I jumped back up to my feet and assumed a fighting stance. Cynem lunged at me, swinging his arm. I dodged it at the last second and kicked him in his abdomen with my knee. He didn't even flinch, throwing his fist against my face again.

This time, I grabbed it. I squeezed his fist until it hurt him. His body crumbled slightly, but he wasn't one to give up in the first moments of a fistfight. He pressed his foot against my belly and launched himself up, doing a backflip.

I never thought that he'd learn how to fight.

He landed on the floor heavily as his fur started to show and his canines grew bigger. I was holding back. I didn't want to transform right now. I didn't want to kill this guy, no matter how much of a threat he was.

I dodged out of the way when he lunged again, landing with a thud on the floor. Scrambling back to my feet, I let out all the air in my lungs when I found him slamming me against the floor.

My blood was cold until now, but he was forcing my hand and I needed to transform until it was too late. And so I did, letting my claws come out and slashing at his chest. He shrieked when he felt his skin opening. I pressed my foot against him and threw him across the room with enough force to make his body thud against the closet.

Cynem hit his head against the hardwood and fell down on the floor, his head hanging from one side. I stood up slowly, wondering if he was going to get back up. But the seconds passed and nothing happened, and I had more pressing matters to tend to.

I went to the bed, looked underneath it with my hand, and snatched what I was looking for. My shotgun. It would come in handy if someone else was also looking out to kill me.

I picked up my phone as I got on Destiny. Time to tell the president what happened and why I was going to need his help.

CHAPTER 12

Nefion

"**S**o, you really left him because you thought you weren't ready for it?" Bren asked, looking at me with judging and kind eyes. He was supporting me. It didn't matter what he thought was going on in my mind when everything went downhill. He was going to support me all the way, which made me realize that, at the end of the day, he was my only friend.

"I just felt so overwhelmed by it all," I replied, wishing things were different. I wished that I was okay with the pregnancy and the fact that I was going to be a father.

I wasn't going to lie. Even though I thought I wasn't sure about it in the beginning, the months that I spent with Palio were more than enough to change my mind. I loved him. It was something I thought I would never say about anyone. Love wasn't something I could control.

I kept saying to myself that I was going to focus on my career and how important college was to me, but I realized that those things didn't matter as much. What mattered was making sure that I was happy with myself and my life.

Now that a couple days had already passed since I left our house, I couldn't help but feel that I made another mistake. It was one thing walking out of the house and leaving him behind, and another to be living away from him and without all the comfort he could give me.

Bren put his hand on mine, caressing it.

"I went through something similar. I'm Cogwyn's fated mate, as you know. The biggest difference is that he also never believed in it. We had to run away from the Bear Bikers in our city. He was all the way with me, always protecting me. Palio's been doing something similar for you, hasn't he?"

His question was genuine, and he was right about that, too.

I looked down, feeling shame overwhelming my heart. I couldn't control it. I just kept making one bad decision after the other, even though I realized I wouldn't have come to that conclusion if I wasn't here.

"Maybe I should talk to him again. Do you think he will forgive me?" I asked, looking at his eyes and finding the same kindness from before.

He nodded slowly, grabbing my hand and standing up with me.

"I did even worse things to Cogwyn and we're still together, as you can see."

As he finished saying that, Cogwyn appeared from behind him and wrapped his arms around his chest, kissing the nape of his neck. It was so reminiscent of the mornings and the nights I had with my husband, who I was very sure was desperate and searching for me.

"You're going to be okay. If you need my help, I'll be there to help you," Cogwyn promised, making me feel so happy that I had their support, no matter what happened. It was so great to know that I had true friends that cared about me. They were so different from the assholes that always wanted to hang out with me, but were never available when I needed them.

I rubbed my hands over my face as I tried to make my mind about it.

There was no denying it. I needed to go see my husband and tell him about everything that happened.

I turned, announcing the news to Bren and Cogwyn when I heard the engine of a motorcycle in the distance. For the first few seconds, I didn't think much of it. Some motorcycles were very loud and we were relatively close to a very busy freeway. Sometimes, we could hear motorcycles riding on it.

But then I noticed that something was different about that engine. I knew that sound. I knew it like the back of my hand.

It was Palio's motorcycle, Destiny. I could still remember how I felt when I first got on it.

Out of the trees and shrubs he came, riding on the motorcycle and pulling up by the front of Bren's house. He had his helmet on, which was something he was still working on. He said that it was just his custom. He didn't like wearing helmets, and I convinced him about the importance of putting them on.

Even though it was a surprise that he found out I was here, I was worried. I thought he was going to flip out at me. There was a good chance he might. After all, I abandoned him without telling him anything about the truth. I hid the truth from him and he should be angry at me, even though I knew he wasn't going to be.

"Nefion, why did you do this?" He asked, throwing his arms around me after rushing over, ignoring the couple behind me. He hugged me so tightly I felt all the air going out of my lungs.

I missed this. I never thought that I would be saying this, but I missed being hugged by my husband and it was so splendid that he was here. I thought I was going to have to go back to our house and do this without the support of Bren and Cogwyn, and I was happy that things were happening differently.

My face still buried on his chest, I said, "I'm so sorry. I was so overwhelmed by it all."

He put his hands on my shoulders, pushing me so that I was looking at his face. His eyes were watery. He was crying, which was something I never thought I would be seeing him doing one day.

"What happened? Did someone kidnap you? Did these people

hurt you?" He said, throwing his finger at Cogwyn. "If they did, I don't know what I'll do, but it won't be nice."

I stepped to stand between him and Cogwyn and Bren, shaking my hands in front of me. "It's nothing like that." I turned my head to look at them, opening a very weak smile on my face.

"They helped me. I needed somewhere to stay for a couple days until I figured out what I wanted, and they were willing to host me. I even cared for their baby once when I was younger."

It was cold here, as it always was. The place was covered in snow. Everything was white and so beautiful, too. I never said this to Palio, but one of the things I wanted to do was to live in a very similar place. Did I think it could be made real? I didn't know, but I could bring that up to Palio.

His expression softened up when he realized that I wasn't lying.

He lowered his eyes before locking them with mine. "You should've told me about this. You should've told me everything. You should never hide anything from me."

I wrung my hands. "I know. There's just something important I need to tell you."

"And you should keep your ears perked up for it. It's the biggest news of your life," Cogwyn said, still hugging his husband from behind. They were like the perfect couple and I wanted to be more like them. Everything was becoming much clearer to my eyes. I wanted to be like them because it was what would make me happy.

I grabbed his hand, feeling how big and heavy it was. My hand was tiny in comparison.

"I told you about it in the letter. I'm not sure if I made it pretty clear, but I really am pregnant and I know that the baby is yours. I didn't even plan for it, which is one of the biggest reasons why I left you. It was overwhelming. My whole life was going to change and I didn't know how to deal with it."

He hugged me tightly again, burying his face in the crook of my neck.

"I'm so happy for you and us. It's good that you're telling me this in person. When I read your letter, I didn't believe it."

And now I realized that I wanted to be together with him for the rest of my life.

CHAPTER 13

Palio

I opened the door of the house, wondering if I was going to find that asshole still around here. I checked out the living room, then the bathroom and the kitchen and the bedroom, not finding him anywhere. Feeling a little relieved, I was pretty sure that that hadn't been the last time I saw him. Cynem would show up again eventually and when he did, I'd be ready for him.

I already told the president about what happened. He'd sort things out. The guy was on the run, but with all of the Wolf Bikers gunning for him, he wasn't going to last much longer. I was sure about that and was salivating.

I closed the door of the bedroom, pushing Nefion against the wall. He moaned softly, locking his eyes with me as he asked, "What were you looking for when you opened the door? It almost looked like you were hunting for something."

"Cynem. He was here looking for a fight. I knocked him out cold and then went out searching for you."

"Cynem..." He looked down, sounding almost sad about it. "I don't know what happened to him, but he lost his way. I never thought that he'd be one to pick a fight."

"Well, he won't survive much longer out there. The Wolf Bikers are looking for him and they'll sniff him out. When that happens... I don't like thinking about it, but they don't treat traitors kindly. He should never have tried to kill me. The president and the rest of the club will never forgive him."

After a moment of silence, Nefion asked, "Can you do a favor for me?"

I smiled, knowing that he was pregnant and that I couldn't do anything he didn't want. After all, I'd do anything to make sure the baby was happy, and it didn't matter the cost of that. Nothing and no one would stand in our way.

"Ask the pack not to hurt him. I want to talk to him in person and show him that he really can't have me anymore. I know why he's acting like this and doing these things. He's so in love with me that he can't stop thinking about me, and that's something I can relate with."

I groaned, the first thought that came into my mind that I should really do that. After all, I needed to make sure that Nefion thought I was always on his side, no matter what.

I lifted his chin, saying, "Fine. I'll do it."

"And tell them that keeping him alive is the most important thing they can do. I don't want them to hurt or kill him, and it's not about how I feel about it, even though I would never forgive myself if they did that. I know he has a good heart."

"Fine. I promise, dear," I murmured, sealing our lips again and rubbing them together, making him moan. Pressing his body against the wall, I couldn't help but lift his shirt and take it off.

After spending days without my husband, there were a lot of things I wanted to do with him and this was just one of them.

He parted his lips, allowing my tongue into his mouth. I battled against his tongue for a little while, winning control over the fight seconds later. Nefion was melting in my arms and I was loving the way he was doing that. As an Omega, he was so submissive.

Our kiss was very passionate and slow, and I could keep on kissing him for hours on end. It did feel like hours were passing even though it was just seconds.

When he pulled his head back, he was breathless. His eyes

were locked with mine and he was telling me so many things through them.

His hands roamed over my body, going down and finding my belt. He smiled without showing his teeth as he undid it and took it off. It fell to the floor, my dick hard and raging. I wanted to be inside of him. I wanted to knot my Omega, and I was pretty sure he was thinking the same.

When he regained his composure and was breathing more normally, he got on his knees and lowered my pair of briefs. The look in his eyes was telling me everything. He was loving what he was seeing. My dick was hard and pointing at him, pre-come seeping out of the slit.

He didn't say it, but the look on his face was more than telling. He missed my cock.

He looped his fingers around it slowly, as if he was afraid of what might happen. He started to pump my cock over and over. When he had his fill of that, he started to play with my balls, loving how warm they were.

I took a step toward him, sliding my cock between his lips. They were very warm and welcoming, and I couldn't see myself doing anything different. For a moment, I really thought I had lost him, but now I realized it was nothing more than a bad dream and that it would never happen again.

I grabbed his hair and started to move his head up and down along my cock, loving the way he was deep-throating me without gagging. He learned so much about sex it was impressive. I taught him so much and now I was reaping the benefits.

He pulled back, kissing the tip of my cockhead when he had his fill of it, too.

His lips were wet and covered with my pre-come, and he wasn't ashamed of that. If anything, he was proud of it.

Nefion then stood up, kissed me again, his hand roaming over my body as he took off my leather jacket. I let him do it. He needed to feel more of me and he was going to get everything he craved.

Our bodies were so hot we were already sweating, even though it was cold outside and we could already see snowflakes falling from the sky.

This afternoon was perfect for what we were doing, the sun falling behind the houses and casting different shades of orange and gold.

I snuck my fingers under my white shirt, lifting it up and over my head. I tossed it to the side, where it couldn't bother us. As soon as Nefion's eyes danced over what his mind had been thinking about this whole time, he took a deep breath.

He didn't need to say it, but he loved my chest. It was built like a tank, covered by scars and tattoos. He moved his right hand over it, stopping at my nipple before he said, "This almost feels like a dream. I'm so glad it is not."

"No, it really isn't," I murmured, scratching his chin and pecking his lips again, feeling so hard right now it was almost impossible to not just bend him over and fuck him until I was knotting him.

I could feel my eyes changing, my wolf side wanting to come out. It wasn't going to. I was keeping it at bay.

He twisted my right nipple and then dove his head, wrapping his lips around it. I groaned, closing my eyes and putting both of my hands on the back of his head. I kept it where I wanted it, his lips working my nipples as his hand continued to jack me off.

Gosh, I missed this so much.

My breathing was quickening when he went for my other nipple, his hand going up and down along my dick, pulling at the skin. I was doing everything in my power not to come right now. I'd only do that when I was inside of him and murmuring that he was the love of my life.

Seconds later, he pulled his head back again and kissed me one more time, grabbing my hand and leading me into our bedroom.

He pushed me down against the bed and laid me on it. I spread my arms around him, pulled him to me, and made out with him for what felt like an eternity, flipping around when the time was right for the thing I'd been most waiting for.

Knotting him again.

I took off the rest of his clothes in a hurry, tossing them over my head. I didn't need to glance down at his butt to know that he was wet and already waiting for me.

I curled up the side of my lips slightly, lining up my shaft to his orifice and breaking in. When I was inside of him, I started to roll my hips and grew bigger as my orgasm surged. I was knotting him, coming inside his tunnel for what felt like an eternity.

I pulled out moments later, falling onto the bed heavily and bringing him to me with my arms. I kissed the side of his neck, cocooning him in arms before murmuring into his ears, "You're the most important person in the world for me. Don't you ever forget that."

"I won't," he replied gently before closing his eyes and falling asleep with me.

While I couldn't sleep and feel rested right now – there was still the matter of Cynem to resolve – we could spend the rest of the day and the night together, not thinking about anything that didn't involve only us.

And then, tomorrow morning, we'd settle the score with Cynem.

CHAPTER 14

Cynem

I cracked my eyes open, realizing that nothing changed since yesterday. I was still with my lover and, this time, he was by my side. I could hear his soft snoring and it was very relieving. He was with me. He didn't flee from me like last time and would never try the same again.

I groaned gently, pushing myself off the bed as I put on a pair of trousers. I looked behind me to make sure that my Omega was still sleeping, and I smiled when I realized he was. He was with his arm hanging from the bed, drooling from one of the sides of his mouth.

Satisfied with what I was seeing, I went to the kitchen and started preparing something nice for him. I knew that this morning he was going to wake up with his belly hungry and begging for food. We had been living long enough for me to know what his food tastes were like, and I was keeping that in mind as I turned on the flames of the stove.

I opened the open, grabbed the pots and pans I was going to need, and then went to the fridge. I popped the door open, took all the other things I was going to need, and then went to the kitchen island. I was going to make bacon, eggs, pancakes, and a lot of other things for my beloved.

My Omega was going to be so hungry he was going to eat all

that and a lot more, too. Thinking that, I was keeping in mind that I needed to excel this time. I needed to be better than my usual self and make the best homemade breakfast he ever had.

I was in front of the stove and dealing with the pans when I heard footsteps approaching the kitchen. It could only be one person, so I was already opening my smile when I saw that it was him. Nefion was in the doorway, supporting his weight against it.

He rubbed the sides of his eyes before saying, "Good morning! It smells very nice what you are making."

I adjusted my apron, going to him after rounding the kitchen island. I wrapped my arms around him, kissed him again, and then looked at his eyes. Even though he was kind of sleepy, he was showing me how happy he was with the way things turned out.

"Hungry?" I asked, pulling one of the chairs so that he could sit on it. He had to put on his clothes before coming to the kitchen as did I before starting to make the breakfast proper. Even though it was nice to be naked inside my own house whenever I wanted, there were times when I needed to do things – like making breakfast – which required my full attention.

I wasn't a cook and I sure as hell wasn't good at cooking, but I was making an exception for my fated Omega.

"Yes. I'm so fucking hungry," he replied, giving me the confirmation I was looking for. I was pretty sure that it didn't matter if I fucked up or not, he was going to love the breakfast I was finishing regardless.

I smiled, went back to the stove, turned off the flames, and then prepared a plate for him. After putting the cutlery he was going to need, he grabbed them and dug in, smiling without showing his teeth.

I was a little nervous. It wasn't the first time he was eating something I whipped up, but it didn't matter. My heart was always tight whenever he was eating something I made.

Wringing my hands, he took another bite of the bacon and eggs, widening his soft smile.

"It's very delicious. Thank you for this. Thank you for being with me, even though I know I fucked up."

I went behind him, settled my hands on his shoulders, and kissed his cheek.

"Don't worry about it. I know you did it thinking about what was best for me and you. I don't hold it against you."

"I'm so lucky to have you," he said and we kept chatting until we both finished our breakfasts. I did the dishes, dried my hands, and then went with him to our bedroom. He was opening his backpack when I hugged him from behind, pressing my groin against his ass.

"I missed you so much. Could you not go to college today?" I asked, hoping that he was going to concede. "I know I'm being selfish, but it's the way I am. I'm jealous. I'm obsessed with you and want to make sure that you are happy. I can only do that when you are with me."

Nefion turned around in my arms, putting his hands on my waist.

"I'm going to think about that. I can't make any promises, though."

"Now you're just teasing me."

He pressed his finger against his lips and then lowered his hand, smiling gently.

"Fine. I won't do that, but we need to do something else to fill up the time. We had breakfast and it was really delicious. Now we need to have something equally tasty."

I studied his eyes, reading what he was thinking.

When Nefion was in the mood, it was impossible not to do what he wanted.

"And what's that?" I purred, moving against his body and feeling how small he was. I thought that this morning we weren't going to do anything sexy, but I realized I was wrong about that. My body was begging for this.

"You know what I'm talking about."

And I did. I didn't need him to say anything else. I just dove in, sealing our lips one more time. We were kissing again and just like all the other times, there was something different about it. Every time we made out, we understood each other better.

We broke the kiss with a plop, his lips refusing to disconnect from mine.

Just like all the other times, he was breathless and I knew he needed more. An Omega like him would never be satisfied with just one kiss, and I was sure he was thinking the same way.

I moved my hand down, cupping his bulge as I started to massage it. He groaned, lying down on the bed as I started to lower his pants. Then, I got rid of his pair of boxer briefs and was all over his shaft.

As a morning gift, I was going to make him come in my mouth.

Without a second thought, I got on my knees and put my fingers around his cock. Not as big as mine, but this wasn't about his size. It was all about bringing him as much pleasure as he could feel, and it was working.

Sliding my hand up and down over his shaft, I worked it, making it a little harder than it was. His cockhead was bulbous and purple-ish, pre-come leaking out of it.

I couldn't help but stick my tongue out and lap it up, his body shaking in pleasure. When I had my fill of that, I kissed the tip of his dickhead – just like he did for me that time – and then sides of his shaft, loving its girth and length.

Gosh, I could spend all day doing this.

Satisfied with that, I snuck one of his balls into my mouth and started to apply pressure on it. Swirling my tongue around it, I felt his body growing hotter, the need to orgasm becoming clearer.

He tilted his head backward and shut his eyes. As I put his other nut inside my mouth and kneaded his legs, he let out a groan of lust as his dick finally erupted. I tightened my lips around it and locked it where it was, shooting rope after rope of his milk all over my mouth.

I smiled, moving away from it and then lying on the bed with him. His dick was getting softer again and I was sure that he was already planning on what we were going to do tonight.

I had to spend so many days without him that my wish now was to make sex with him all the time, no matter how tired we were.

NEFION'S EPILOGUE

When I woke up, I realized that my husband was already seated on the bed. I thought that it was already nighttime and he was going to prepare dinner for us, but then I realized the sun was still high in the sky and that the light coming through the windows was very bright.

We didn't sleep per se. We only took a very short nap and I wondered why. I always slept a lot when I was okay with everything that was going on in my life. It should be the case now that I made up my mind and decided I wanted to continue being married to him.

I opened and closed my eyes, noticing that he was holding his phone to his ear. He was talking to someone and it looked pretty important. Not only that, but his shoulders looked so tense I was pretty sure it was more than that. He was worried about something.

"I'm on my way," he stated, ending the call and putting his phone back down on the nightstand. I thought he was going to notice that I was already awake, but he didn't. During the next few seconds, he didn't say anything, staring at the closet like something was going to jump out of it.

I cleared my throat gently and he turned around, smiling when he noticed that it was just me.

"I heard what you said. Did something happen?" I asked, hoping that he wasn't going to dance around the question.

He put his hand on my thigh, saying, "I think I've got big news for you."

"What sort of big news?" I asked. The way he was looking at me was making me worried something was up. He wouldn't be awake now if that wasn't the case.

"They got him."

"They got who?"

"Cynem. He's surrounded and the president wants us to go there to talk to him. I think that he's trying to kill himself."

I bulged my eyes, incapable of wrapping my mind around what he just said. I couldn't believe it. The man that was always so strong, so determined about everything, and always certain of his choices was now trying to kill himself? It didn't make sense. And if it did, I would feel terrible about it.

"What happened to him? How did you manage to catch him?"

He got up, put his clothes back on, and replied, "We need to go there right away. I said I'd do whatever was needed to end the problem we have with him and now is the right opportunity for that. Remember that you said you wanted to talk to him in person, too."

"I know and I'm going to. It's just difficult thinking that this is finally going to happen. After he came here and… Kissed me without my consent, I thought I would never be able to forgive him."

Hearing that, Palio pushed himself away from me, driving his hand over his face.

"I was ready to do the same for him, but please don't tell me he really did that."

Realizing the mistake I just made, I knew there was no going back. My husband wanted to know the whole truth and that was it. It was part of the truth and it couldn't be omitted.

I stepped toward him, putting a hand on his shoulder. He had his back turned to me, like he was doing everything in his power to hide what his face was showing. It wasn't like it was working, though. I could feel how tense his shoulder was. If it were possible, he would snap Cynem's neck, and that was putting it mildly.

"I never told you about it, but it did happen and, for what it's worth, I didn't like it."

He lifted his hand, fisting it.

"It's unforgivable. He knew you were married to me. He crossed a line that should never have been crossed."

"I know you're right and I don't ask for your forgiveness. I just hope you understand. I never thought Cynem was like that too, but he showed that he is someone different. He has some issues he needs to deal with and we need to prove that we are better than him."

He opened his hand, lowering his arm. Turning around so that his eyes were seeing me, he took a deep breath and appeared to be calming down.

"You're probably right, my love," he said, kissing my lips softly and going for his helmet. He picked it up, opened the door of the garage, and I sat down on it.

He helped me put on my helmet, which was such a significant progress for him that I was impressed by it. Little by little, Palio was learning the importance that came with protecting ourselves when he was riding his motorcycle.

He twisted the handlebars and we rode off, arriving at the destination moments later. A crowd was already gathering by the front of the building. When I looked up, I spotted what I was looking for. Cynem and a bunch of other bikers, including the president, standing by the edge of the roof of the building.

He had his gun pointed to his face and was threatening to kill himself if they continued to approach him. I didn't need to be right there with them to know what was going on in his mind.

He wasn't pulling our leg. He wasn't trying to fool us. If the bikers took another step toward him, he would kill himself.

It was just crazy that, this whole time, I never noticed that he had mental issues. I knew he was obsessed with me, that he had an uncontrollable crush on me, but I never thought it was so crippling.

I got off the bike and went to the elevator of the building. Palio was right behind me as I pressed the button to go to the roof. The elevator doors opened and we jumped out, finding ourselves where everyone else was.

As we stepped toward them, the president of the biker club turned his head to look at us. I didn't need to look at his eyes to know what he was thinking. He was confused about everything and wanted to put an end to it his own way. Problem was, I wasn't going to let that happen.

I stepped through the crowd as I found myself a couple of feet in front of Cynem.

"Cynem, what the hell do you think you're doing? You're better than this."

"I was wrong about it."

"About what?" I asked, feeling confused as well.

"About who killed my parents. It wasn't Palio."

I scrunched up my eyebrows. I could grasp what was going on in his mind. This whole time, he put the blame on Palio, but it turned out he didn't have anything to do with it. I was already feeling more relieved. I never forgot about that, but it was good to know it was never a problem.

"You should be happy. You are admitting that you made a mistake."

"But there's a problem with that."

"And what problem is that?" I asked, stepping toward him as I tested the waters. I was wondering if he could really do it. I was almost sure he couldn't kill himself because it was me this time, and it appeared that I was right. He didn't pull the trigger now.

He pointed with his head toward the president, replying, "It was the president. This whole time, I whored myself for him, trying to do everything to please him, and even joined the pack, but I made a mistake. He was only using me. He was the one who killed my parents."

Palio turned his head to look at him, arching his eyebrows.

"Is it true? Were you really in the war?"

The president waved his hand, narrowing his eyes.

"I never told you, but I was. I just thought that it didn't matter. It was such a long time ago."

"You should have told us. Everyone here deserved to know it."

"I suppose you're right. I don't care about it. I just want this shit to be over."

I stepped toward Cynem, grabbed the hand that was holding the pistol, lowered it and then stepped away from the edge of the roof with him.

When it was clear that he wasn't going to kill himself anymore, I heard a collective sigh of relief around me. He was still shedding tears when he lamented, "I don't know what to do anymore. I don't want to be a biker, I don't want to be in college, and nobody loves me."

I didn't know what to do, either, but I couldn't abandon him. Even though it wasn't my responsibility, I was going to find a new goal for his life.

PALIO'S EPILOGUE

I was in the hospital, pacing from side to side in front of the door. Months after what happened on the roof of that building, I could say that I certainly felt much better about what happened. We found a place for Cynem, the guy I couldn't stand.

My progress in terms of feeling empathy was astounding. My whole life, I thought that I only cared about myself and finding my mate. I thought that nobody else mattered to me, but then I realized there was more to life than that.

It was one of the reasons why I was also worried about the fate of my baby. They were still performing the operation and the room was so small, especially for someone my size.

My friends from the biker club were worried about what was going to happen as well. They were with me in the hallway, looking confused and uncomfortable.

They wanted to step up and help me figure things out, but they couldn't. Many of them hadn't found their mates yet, after all.

The president was also here with me, though our friendship was already cracked. What was revealed during the incident a couple of months ago was forever going to remain in my mind. I was sure of that and couldn't stop thinking about it every time I looked at him.

"You should calm down. It's going to be fine, really. This is one of the best hospitals in the city and the doctors and nurses are professionals."

"I know, but it doesn't matter. Nefion needs me right now. He needs me holding his hand, telling him over and over that everything will be alright."

He shrugged, shaking his head. "Well, you know that can't happen. That's what the doctors and nurses said. Not to mention that you take up too much space in the room."

Everyone laughed out loud at that and I even tried to smile, but this was no time for jokes. I was so worried that I felt like my body was wrong and that I shouldn't be in it.

Then, one of the nurses opened the door and announced, "You can come in, but only you."

I looked at everyone that was in the hallway and I was happy when I got their nods of confirmation. I went into the room, pushed past the doctors and the nurses, and went to where my lover was. In his arms was the most beautiful and tiniest thing in the world.

I was already by their side when he said, "I saw you outside so grumpy and worried. That was so you."

I didn't know what to do. I knew that I had always worked toward this moment, but I didn't know what I'd do when it was actually happening. I was a father now and I had a baby. It was a baby boy.

"He's an omega, just like me," Nefion said, almost as if he was reading my mind.

My baby was an Omega? It was like a dream come true. I mean, I'd have been equally happy if he was an alpha, but there was just something different knowing that he was an Omega.

"You look surprised. I mean, he was always either going to be an Alpha or an Omega, or maybe a Beta."

I knew what was going on in his mind. If our baby was a Beta, there would be problems. Betas were looked down on in our society, more so than the Bikers. They were the middle term between an Omega and an Alpha, and they usually didn't mingle with us.

They lived isolated in some of the most violent neighborhoods in the city, where they usually chose the life of becoming a Bear Biker, if they were shifters like me.

I pushed those thoughts out of my mind. They had no place in it right now.

"Do you want to hold him?" Nefion queried, smiling softly.

Knowing that I couldn't say no, I picked up the baby and held him in my arms. I didn't know how I was supposed to hold him properly, if I was doing this right or was hurting him.

"It's okay. You're doing it right. When you get used to it, it will feel like you've been doing it for all of your life," Nefion said, noticing how uncomfortable I looked right now.

The baby was tiny, making me wonder how it was that something like this could grow into a full man.

"Here, do this," Nefion said, rubbing the tip of the little one's nose until he opened his eyes and looked at me. I didn't know if he knew that I was his father, but I liked to think that, deep in his mind, he was already aware of it.

He started to wave his arms in the air, as if he was trying to grab me. I didn't know what to do right now.

"Show him your finger. He's going to love it," Nefion said, doing just that so that I knew how to do it.

After he retracted his hand, I showed the little one our finger and he moved his hands as if he was trying to grab it. I didn't know if he was going to manage to, but he was still moving his hands in such a cute way I couldn't help but blush.

Moments later, when I thought that it was already a lost cause, he managed to latch his hands around my finger and tug at it. He was quite strong, I noticed. I didn't think that someone so tiny could already grip so firmly.

Then, he started to giggle before letting go of my finger.

"Looks like he's already bored of it. Don't worry. He's like that, I think," Nefion said, offering me his arms. He was asking me to give the baby back to him, which I did. When our little one wasn't in my arms anymore, I felt like something important was missing. I wanted to be holding him for all of eternity.

There were going to be plenty of opportunities for that, I reminded myself.

"He's our little Rein," he said, mentioning the name we chose for our little one. It took us a lot of time, but we managed to find a name that stirred some reaction from Rein when he was still in my lover's belly.

"Yes, he is," I said, kissing the side of his cheek, pulling over a chair, and sitting on it. I took his hand, holding it. "And he will have the best life possible. When you're out of college and working, we'll be making more money than we know what to do with it."

He chuckled as one of the nurses approached us. "We need to take Rein to the nursery, if you don't mind," she said and I sighed. I looked at my husband's eyes, giving him the confirmation he was looking for. He wasn't going to be able to see his son for a while, which sucked, but there wasn't much he could do about it.

"I suppose it can't be helped," he said, holding out the baby and giving it to the nurse.

She put it in her arms and said, "Thanks. Don't worry. You'll be given the green light soon and then you'll be able to go home."

"I'll take plenty of pictures," I offered, giggling with him.

His eyes contemplated me and he then put his hand on my cheek, kissing me moments later. It was a short, passionate kiss that sent goosebumps all over my body. The rest of my life was going to be like this? I asked myself, already knowing the answer.

Of course it was going to be.

"I love you so much," I said and we kissed again, knowing that only good things awaited us.

The End

This was book 3. The first two stories of the series can be

found here:

1. Omega for Obsessive Alpha

2. Omega for Protective Alpha

Lastly, leave a review if you liked the book. It always helps me so much!

SNEAK PEEK: OMEGA FOR OBSESSIVE ALPHA

Wolf Shifter MPREG Fated Mates Romance (Omegaverse MC - 1)

Feran

I felt something sniffing me, like he was trying to smell me. I cracked open my eyes as I found someone standing right in front of me. It was a man, huge, older than me, and hot as balls. The moment my eyes set on him, it was like fireworks exploded in my head.

I wanted to rip his clothes off his body and see what he was like naked. I wanted to slide my tongue over his muscles, to feel him for the man he was, to grind my body against his, and to make sweet love with him. I was already drooling even though I didn't even notice that yet.

The guy who was in front of me was so close I could smell the minty odor coming out of his mouth. His eyes were emerald green, his hair messy and blond, some stubble on his chin. His face was chiseled and followed hard lines, making me want to put my hand on it and feel it until he was smiling.

"

And I just noticed I was supposed to be falling to the floor.

I felt something holding me in place so that that didn't happen. It was his arm, wrapped around my torso. It was firm, showing off his confidence. I was still in the same room from before, which was behind the bar where I was drinking away my sorrows.

I just remembered something terrible that happened not too long ago, which made me come running to this place. I supposed I should be thankful he was holding me like this so that I didn't fall and hurt myself, but the way he was smelling me was also frightening and annoying. I should be shoving him away from me as fast as possible and as hard as I could, but that was easier said than done.

I wasn't going to say that I was skinny. In fact, I was lean and I did work out, but I didn't follow any diet and I didn't inject my body with anything. This guy, on the other hand, looked more like a gym rat than anything.

And he was even more frightening because his body was covered in tattoos. There was even one of them, which caught my attention the most, sneaking from under his shirt and going across his neck. It was the tattoo of a lone wolf, making me remember that he was probably from *that* MC gang. I shivered at the thought of having caught the attention of one of them. It was the worst thing that could be happening.

Not to mention that I didn't have anything to do with him...

He parted his lips, blowing a bigger cloud of his mouth's odor over my face. I closed my eyes and scrunched up my nose, but not because I was turned off by the smell, but because his scent was overwhelming.

As an Omega, I was always subjected to this kind of situation, especially when the other guy was an Alpha. And it wasn't just the smell coming out of his mouth that was making me hard and aroused right now. It was also his musky scent, which came from all around his body.

"I just saved you from hurting yourself. I think you should be thanking me." And as soon as he finished saying that, he smiled, showing me his perfect teeth. I always thought that bikers like him didn't brush their teeth, but it looked like he was an exception.

I knew he was a biker because of the patch he had on the front of his leather jacket. It showed that he, indeed, was from one of the biker gangs in the region. They were called the Wolf Bikers, and everyone around here in the city feared them. They were a menace, robbing people and their houses, causing the police all sorts of troubles.

I knew that coming to this bar was a mistake, but I didn't think I was going to run into a member of the Wolf Bikers.

I shot my hands to his chest, shoving them against it. I thought he was going to leave me alone and add some distance between us, but he held his ground, tightening how hard his arm was pressing against my torso...

Yel

I stomped hard onto the grass, my fangs growing bigger. Fisting my hand, I couldn't help but feel like punching that bear biker until blood was gushing out of his mouth. I was going to bash his head against the pavement until his skull cracked, I swore.

I couldn't believe I was so amateur about it. I should have realized someone was going to come after him, too. I was going to make bank by kidnapping Feran.

Stomping on the grass again, all I could do was turn back and stride over to Delight, my bike. It was parked in front of the bar. The members of the Wolf Bikers didn't know that I was here. They didn't frequent this part of town. I was the only one here, and the only one who should have known about Feran.

He was from one of the most important families in the city. I knew that kidnapping him would make me a lot of money. I didn't even feel bad about it, and I wouldn't either way. The money his family would have to hand over wouldn't even dent their fortune, after all.

I couldn't lose this opportunity.

The moon high above the buildings and the houses, I looked up at it as I realized how easy it would have been to turn into a wolf while that Bear Biker was pointing his gun in my direction. In a fair fight, did he think he would win?

Fuck that guy. He'd always been a nuisance. He was keeping tabs on me.

Ennith…

I was going to punch his gut so hard one day he would puke whatever was in his stomach, I swore, swinging my leg over Delight and remembering all the things that happened between us. All the clashes we had, even when he was in school and trying to prove to the teachers he was better than me at pretty much anything. He joined up with the Bears because they were the right fit for him.

Turning on the engine of the motorcycle and propelling it forward, crossing one red traffic light after the other without even putting on my helmet, I was focused on just one thing – finding Ennith and Feran. I was pretty sure I knew where he was taking him to.

The Bear Bikers' hideout.

It wasn't too far and even though I wasn't going to have the support of the Wolf Bikers, I should be okay. I didn't need them, anyway. I was pretty confident in how well I could sneak in and out of that place. It was pretty big, with ample free space. I was going to have to keep my guard up all the time, but it wasn't a challenge impossible to tame.

I smirked, feeling overconfident. I had my gun with me now.

I'd left it in the motorcycle because I didn't think I was going to have to use it during the kidnapping. I thought it was going to be simple. Feran was pretty small, a little lean, weak, and very submissive. Me being the Alpha I was, he was always going to smell me and fall to his knees when his nose got a sniff of it. I mean, everything was going according to plan before Ennith popped up.

I couldn't help but feel aroused by Feran, though. He had short, dark hair, perfect lips, ocean-blue eyes, and lips that were just the right size. When I enclosed my arm around his torso, the first thought that popped up in my mind was how much I wanted to rip the clothes off his body and bend him over. It only didn't happen because raping was something I would never do.

He was about 10 years younger than me, too. That was a piece of information I dug out on the internet. And that age gap was a plus for me, too. If we had met under different circumstances, I'd be going for him for sure. The only problem with that was that now he thought of me just as an asshole who was trying to kidnap him.

Being the person I was, I couldn't care less about that.

I pulled up not too far from their hideout, pushing my motorcycle until it was hidden in a dark and forgotten alleyway between two massive buildings. I pulled up my hood, shadowing my face, and went to one of the doors that two guards were by the side of.

Their hands went to their pistols as soon as they realized someone was padding over to them...

MPREG SERIES AND MORE

SERIES - PREGNANT FOR HIM

1. Controlled by the Alpha 1: An MPREG Omegaverse Story
2. Controlled by the Alpha 2: An MPREG Omegaverse Story
3. Controlled by the Alpha 3: Dominating the Fertile Omega
4. Controlled by the Alpha 4: An Omega's Tale of Obedience
5. Controlled by the Alpha 5: A Tale of Obedient Submission
6. Controlled by the Alpha 6: Monopolized in Outer Space

SERIES - LOST INNOCENCE

1. Overwhelming the Omega 1: His Little Doll
2. Overwhelming the Omega 2: Brute Entry and Double Teamed
3. Overwhelming the Omega 3: His Tight Backdoor
4. Overwhelming the Omega 4: Stretching his Front Door
5. Overwhelming the Omega 5: Until he Spasms
6. Overwhelming the Omega 6: Naïve and Untouched

Straight to gay first time bundles:

1. Stuffed by Blue Collars: The Full Straight to Gay Age Gap Story

2. Throbbing Hard: A Straight to Gay MMF Bundle

3. Teasing Older Men: 16 Straight to Gay MM Stories

4. Helping Hand: 13 Forbidden Older Man Stories

5. So BIG It Hurts MEGA Bundle: 14 Stories of Man of the House, Brats and Gay Sitters

ABOUT THE AUTHOR

Michael Levi's biggest passion? Writing steamy, romantic stories that leave his readers panting. He's currently focusing on Omegaverse and Bicurious stories, but his collection is diverse and there are books for everyone's tastes. If you're looking for straight to gay, first time, BBC, sissification, and more, you're going to find them on his author page.

He lives to pamper his readers, every kiss means a lot more than what meets the eye, and he loves his Alpha males. Making sure that every gay first time feels different, Michael Levi writes his stories with a cup of coffee by his side. And for inspiration, he always opens a photo of his new crush.